A Word to Parents and Teachers . . .

THE MAGIC MERRY-GO-ROUND brings your child into the wonderful world of the woodcarver's shop. There were times and places where the carousel, or merry-go-round, figures were carved by craftsmen in their small shops. This story is set somewhere in that time and place.

In the happy story of THE MAGIC MERRY-GO-ROUND, your child will come to understand how to become a Christian. Papa Paus and his puppet present the plan of salvation in simple, easy-to-understand terms.

Printed in the United States of America

THE MAGIC MERRY-GO-ROUND

by V. Gilbert Beers

Illustrated by Suzanne Carlton

THE SOUTHWESTERN COMPANY

Nashville, Tennessee

"Who else could make such wonderful things?" said Eric. "You are the best woodcarver in the world, Papa Paus. There is magic in your fingers."

The old woodcarver smiled and wrinkled his nose. "When you grow older, you will make better things than these merry-go-round horses," he said.

"Only if you keep on showing me what to do," Eric said. "Will you, Papa Paus, please?"

The old man frowned and the twinkle went from his eyes. "If only I could," he answered. "But I must tell you something that your friends do not know. I must soon close this shop. Mr. Grumph is very angry at me. He will not rent the building to me any more."

"Why?" Eric asked angrily. "When will he do this? Where will you go? What will you do?"

"Wait! Wait!" Papa Paus laughed. "One question at a time."

"But he can't do that," Eric shouted. "I want to keep coming here . . . always! So do my friends. We want to watch you carve the horses for the merry-go-round. We want to look at this wonderful little merry-go-round you have made. And we want to hear your stories."

The woodcarver looked sad as he talked. "That is why Mr. Grumph is taking my shop from me," he said. "He thinks my stories are bad for the children. He does not want his own girl, Elsa, to come here again—ever! When I close my shop, I will move to another village. I'm afraid that will be soon, too."

Eric stamped his foot and shouted, "I hate that Mr. Grumph. I hate him! I hate him! Some day I will get even with him!"

A twinkle came back into the old woodcarver's eyes. "Come with me," he said. "I want you to meet a new friend."

Eric looked puzzled as Papa Paus opened the lid of a big chest. "A friend?" he asked. "In there?"

The woodcarver took a puppet from the chest and held him up for Eric to see. "This is our new friend, Glum George," he said. "I made him last week. Would you like to talk with him?"

"Why do you look so sad?" Eric asked the puppet.

"There is something wrong inside my heart," said Glum George. "I keep doing things I should not do. I keep saying things I should not say. Sometimes I even say I hate people."

Eric looked at Papa Paus. "Is something wrong inside my heart, too?" he asked.

"Everyone has something wrong inside his heart until he asks God to change him," said Papa Paus. "This is called sin. Sin makes you unhappy. It makes God unhappy, too. But Jesus died to take that sin out of your heart."

Papa Paus moved the strings on Glum George. The corners of his mouth turned up and a big smile came on his face.

"You're not glum anymore," Eric said to the puppet. "You look glad now."

"This is what happens to people when they ask Jesus to take their sin away and give them a new life," said Papa Paus.

Eric was very quiet as he left Papa Paus' shop. He watched his friends skating on the lake as he walked toward home. He thought of the things that Papa Paus and his puppet had told him, and the things he had heard about Mr. Grumph.

The next morning Eric felt a warm breeze as he walked out of his house. During the night the snow had begun to melt. Little streams ran by the side of the road as he walked toward Papa Paus' shop.

When Eric came near the shop, he saw the woodcarver putting a sign near the lake behind his shop. Eric wondered what the sign said. As he came closer to the shop, he began to run.

"What are you doing?" Eric called. Papa Paus looked up. Then he finished hammering the sign post into the ground.

"It is not safe to skate on the lake today," he said. "I must put up this sign to warn our young friends that the ice is too thin."

Eric followed Papa Paus into the shop. While the woodcarver began to work on the beautiful horse for the merry-go-round, Eric looked again at the small model of the merry-go-round on the table.

"All my life I have dreamed of riding on a real merry-go-round," Eric said. "I had thought that some day you could help me do that. But now . . ."

Eric was afraid to finish. Quietly he walked to the window and stared out at the lake.

"I have been thinking of the things you and the puppet said yesterday," Eric started to say. "I . . ." Eric stopped.

"Papa Paus," he shouted. "A girl is skating on the lake. I must warn her about the thin ice."

Eric put on his heavy coat and ran out the door. The woodcarver followed, pulling on his coat as he ran. But just as he came out into the melting snow, he heard Eric cry out.

"Papa Paus! Papa Paus! She has fallen in!"

The woodcarver ran into the shop and came back quickly with a big coil of rope. When he reached the shore of the lake, he threw one end to the girl in the water.

"Hang on!" Papa Paus cried out. Then he and Eric pulled and tugged until the girl was safely on shore.

When the girl looked up at them, Eric caught his breath. "It's Elsa Grumph!" he whispered.

For some time that morning, Papa Paus sat with Eric and Elsa before the fireplace, waiting for Elsa's clothes to dry. Suddenly Eric turned to Papa Paus. "Tell me more about Glum George and Glad George," he said. "I know that I am doing things that are wrong. I want to know more about the new life from Jesus." Papa Paus was happy, for he wanted Elsa Grumph to hear these things, too.

When Elsa's clothes were dry, the woodcarver hitched up his horses to the sleigh. Then he went toward the Grumph home with Elsa and Eric.

When Mr. Grumph opened his door and saw Papa Paus standing there with Elsa, his face became red and his eyes grew angry. "I told you to stay away from Elsa," he shouted. "I don't want her listening to your . . ."

"But Father," Elsa interrupted. "He saved my life this morning. He and Eric pulled me from the lake." Then she told all that had happened.

Mr. Grumph looked down. He could not let his eyes look at Papa Paus. At last he spoke softly. "Come in, please," he said. "We must talk about some things."

"While I am here," said Papa Paus, "I will tell you that next Monday will be my last day at the shop. I will finish the merry-go-round horses and take them to the city. Then I plan to live in the city."

"No!" shouted Eric. "You can't!"

"I'm afraid that won't do," said Mr. Grumph, ignoring Eric's interruption.

Papa Paus looked surprised. "But I can't leave any earlier," he said. "I must finish carving the horses."

"You don't understand," said Mr. Grumph. "You should not leave the village. I was wrong in wanting you to leave. The children would miss you. I want you to stay there in your shop."

Eric and Elsa looked at each other. Then they began to laugh happily. They ran to Papa Paus and threw their arms around him.

Papa Paus began to laugh, too, as he put his arms around the two. Then he was quiet for a moment. "Why didn't I think of this before," he said. "I will take you two with me to the city. You can watch the men put the merry-go-round together. Perhaps they will even let you ride on it."

Then the woodcarver turned to Mr. Grumph. "Would you mind?" he said. "I will ask Eric's parents, too."

Mr. Grumph looked happy for the first time. "If I were younger, I would go, too," he said. "Of course, Elsa may go with you."

When the day came to go to the city, Papa Paus carefully wrapped the wooden horses and put them in the back of the sleigh. Then he climbed into the front with Eric and Elsa and called to the horses to go.

Eric and Elsa asked Papa Paus many questions on the way to the city. As the sleigh moved swiftly across the snow-covered roads, the three friends talked again about Glad George and the new life they could have from Jesus.

"I want Jesus to give me a new life," said Eric.

"So do I," said Elsa.

"Then why don't we talk about this?" Papa Paus asked. He smiled as he listened to Eric and Elsa talk about Jesus and the new life they wanted from Him. Then they went on toward the city.

The city was a new and exciting place to Eric and Elsa. They watched with fascination as the men put Papa Paus' wooden horses into place on the great merry-go-round. Piece by piece, the wonderful thing became more like the model in Papa Paus' shop.

At last the merry-go-round was finished, and all the workmen stepped back to admire it. "Now we will see if it runs," said the man in charge. "Would you two like to ride on those horses you brought?"

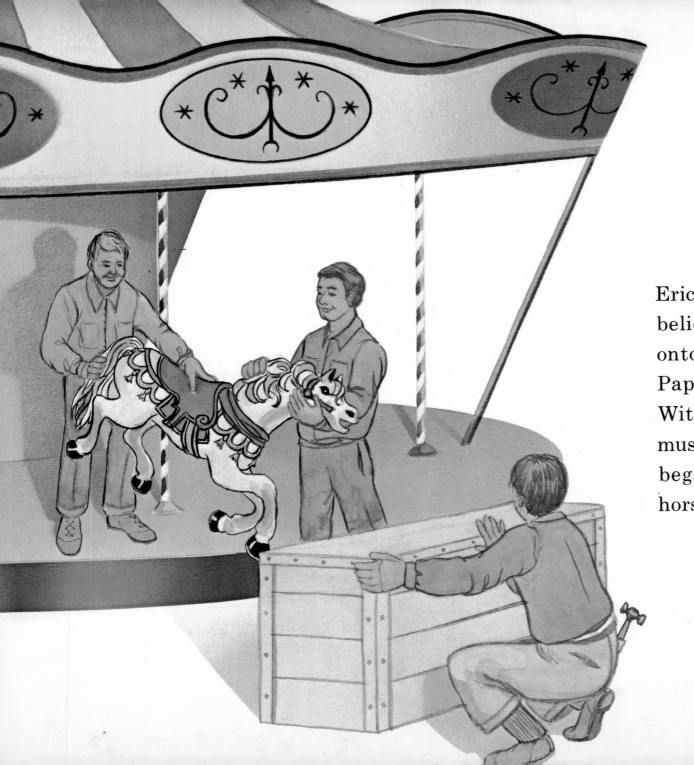

Eric and Elsa could hardly believe it as they climbed onto the two horses which Papa Paus had carved. With a wonderful sound of music the merry-go-round began to move and the horses moved with it.

On and on the two rode, as though caught up in some wonderful, magical place. Eric's dream had come true. For the first time, he was riding on a real merry-go-round. But even better, he was riding with a friend on Papa Paus' wooden horses.

When the merry-go-round stopped, Papa Paus reached up to help the two get off.

"Did you like the ride?" he asked.

Eric's eyes sparkled. "Oh, Papa Paus," he said. "Every time I went around, I thought of the wonderful work you did when you made the horses for this merry-go-round, and of all the children who would ride on them. Papa Paus, please help me become a great woodcarver, just like you."

The woodcarver had an extra bright twinkle in his eyes as he walked to his sleigh with Eric and Elsa. There would be much to talk about on the way home. And there would be many happy days ahead, helping Eric carve some horses for another magic merry-go-round.